T0365168

The Hail Mary

Joseph (Joe Lopez)

authorHOUSE®

AuthorHouse™
1663 Liberty Drive
Bloomington, IN 47403
www.authorhouse.com
Phone: 1-800-839-8640

Published by AuthorHouse   03/19/2012

ISBN: 978-1-4567-4451-9 (sc)
ISBN: 978-1-4567-4450-2 (e)

The church bells rang loud and melodious. People were gathering inside for mass. The church campus ministry was having a special prayer service for the football team. After the service, there would be a huge pep rally at the gym. It was the first time that our school ever made it to the championship game. Expectations were high. We wanted to win it all. Suddenly, the loud roar of a chopper bike muffled the chiming of the church bells. It was the quarterback Jo Cool. He parked his bike and raced across campus to the chapel. He said to the people outside, "Is it over?" The people answered, "No, the service is just about to begin." Jo replied disappointingly, "Aw Shucks!" He sat next to Diesel the running back. At communion time, Diesel said to Jo, "Let's go receive communion." Jo asked, "Don't I have to be a church member to do that?" Diesel answered, "Nah, anybody can take communion." Jo replied, "Well, why is it called the Body & Blood? It must have some significance." Diesel responded, "Well, everybody else is doing it. Come on, it'll be fun. Let's be part of the group." Jo remarked, "I'll pass buddy. You can have mine."

After the service, students and faculty filed into the gym. They all clapped and stomped to the song "We Will Rock You". The dance team performed several numbers. Then, the lights grew dim followed by flashing lights accompanied by a tune for making dramatic entrances. While the music played and lights flashed, the announcer called out the players one by one until he got to the last and most important one of all. He called out, "And last but certainly not least, number five from Hog County, your quarterback and mine, Jo Cool!" Jo high fived his teammates as he took his spot among them. The place shook as the crowd cheered and roared with euphoria. As Jo took his place, the arena grew dark. Then, the spotlight fell on Jo. He stood there being bathed with adoration as the spotlight shined on him.

It was football night at the Cool residence. The guys gathered around the television set to watch the big game. It was the heavily favored Raiders vs. the Cinderella team of the year, the Sentinels. It was a hard fought defensive struggle. Neither team could score. Finally, the Raiders kicked a field goal with just less than two minutes to go in the game. The Sentinel's quarterback, the Rifleman, would have to lead his team, from their twenty, all the way downfield to tie the game or win it with a touchdown. The offense lined up at the line of scrimmage. The Rifleman approached the center to prepare for the snap. Suddenly, Violet cried out, from the kitchen, "Oh My Gosh, my water broke. Damn it! I've gone into labor. Billy get the car. We've got to get to the hospital." Billy got the car, helped Violet in and drove to the hospital. Along the way, he turned on the radio to listen to the game. The announcer called out the action. He said with exuberance, "The Rifleman gets the snap and hands off to Taylor also known as 'The Bulldozer'. No wait! The Rifleman still has the ball. He's running right looking downfield for a receiver. He dodges one tackler. He dodges another. He's almost at the sideline. I hope he doesn't step out of bounds. He pumps once. He pumps twice. He launches the ball deep downfield to Maryweather, the wide receiver, with no time left on the clock. Oh My Gosh! He caught it! I can't believe it! He caught the ball! He's racing to the end zone. Ain't no one gonna catch him now. He's in! He made it! Touchdown! The Sentinels have won in an upset. They're calling it 'The Hail Mary'. What an exciting victory for the Sentinels."

Suddenly, the car screeched to a halt. Billy and Violet arrived at the hospital. Violet was taken inside and prepared for labor. The doctor said to her, "Push Violet, Push!" Violet gave out a loud scream as she pushed. Then, there was the cry of a new born child. He was wrapped in swaddling clothes and given to Violet. The doctor looked at him and said, "He is so cool. Look, what's that on the side of his face? Are those side burns?" Billy looked and said, "Yes, I believe so." The nurse asked, "What's his name? Violet answered, "We'll give him his dad's middle name – Jo." Both the doctor and nurse said, "His name is Jo Cool? That is so cool."

It was nine o'clock. Russell rushed into the conference room. He took a seat with his fellow agents while his boss Ed spoke. He showed a photo of a wanted terrorist. He told the group, "The man in the photo is Hasad Mosheik. He is also known as Mo. Mr. Mosheik is a religious extremist. He has ties to Islam, Buddhism, Confucianism, and even nudism. He's been arrested before for streaking at a football game during halftime chanting, 'Down with American Football'. He's a sick puppy. He belongs to an organization called The Pigskins. Their goal is to destroy everything American especially football. They believe that football is a modern day Zeus who sits on the throne of American commerce. If they can destroy football, so the theory goes, American influence in the world will be broken. With America out of the way, they'll dominate and ultimately control the world."

After a brief moment for questions, Ed, the FBI chief continued, "According to information gathered in the field, we were able to uncover this video. Ed played the video for the agents. It was a video of a football game. It was the Raiders vs. Sentinels nail biter. At the end of the video, Hadan

Mosheik appeared. He said, "Exciting game wasn't it? Imagine life without football. It would be very boring. Wouldn't it? America, without football, would cease to exist. Well, I'm a reasonable man. Just give me Italy with a harem of beautiful girls, a company of hot exotic female dancers and a bank account to keep them happy for a lifetime, and maybe I might not destroy your wonderful country. Twitter me your response. By the way, you can also find me on facebook. I'll see you at the game. Have a splendid day."

Ed looked at the group and said, "You see what I mean? He's a madman. Unfortunately, he's a madman with expertise in explosives. He's also been educated in chemical and biological warfare. Last but not least, he obviously knows a lot about American football. On that note, let me point out the man in charge of this operation." Ed called out, "Russell Shaw, please stand up." Russell stood up. The guys and gals in the room barked and rolled their fists, "Woof! Woof! Woof!" Ed continued, "Okay, settle down everybody. Russell is an ex-ball player. He'll be able to stay one step ahead of this psycho we're trying to catch. We've also brought in an expert on the Middle East. She is agent Bahijah Buhjah. Just call her Bonnie. Bonnie is a native Arabian who happens to speak in a sexy Russian accent. She will be Russell's partner on this mission." Bonnie stood up to address the group. She said, "It won't be easy catching Mosheik. He's a diabolical genius. That is why I must sleep with him. Once I wrap myself around his deliciously crazed body and let him inside, we'll become one. Then, I'll better understand his motives and warped mentality." Kristi said out loud as she scribbled on her notepad, "Someone around here sure is slutty." Bonnie responded annoyingly, "I'm an expert at questioning criminals and gathering information out in the field. I've studied with the K.G.B. and Russian Intelligence. I've had three years of intense training." Kristi replied mockingly, "You Da Ho!" Bonnie replied indignantly in her Russian accent, "I must slap you." Ed interrupted and said, "Settle down everybody. Russian investigators work differently than Americans. Let's work together and stay focused. We're hunting a master criminal. Keep me informed and Good Luck."

Russell and Bonnie got together. Russell

asked her, "Tell me about Mr. Mosheik." Bonnie began, "I met him at King Saud University. He was there on a football scholarship. He had moves that would make any woman stand up and cheer. I would stand on the sideline shaking my pom-poms hoping to get his attention but to no avail. He was too popular. It was there at the university that he met Abdulla Al-Turki. We called him Al. Al was a philosophy student and soon to be expert in religious studies. He taught Mosheik that football was an American influence impressed on people in order to dominate the world. He also introduced him to the elite terrorist group The Pigskins. As part of his initiation, he was to carry out an act of terror on the enemy. Mosheik reasoned that since he was already a football player, he could attack the enemy from within. At the big game against Tel Aviv, he rigged his helmet with an explosive device. It was set to explode at the end of the game. At that time, he would take off the helmet and toss it into the crowd killing as many spectators as possible thus creating terror. However, toward the end of the game, Mosheik lateralled to the running back. As he tried to block, he got hit hard to the ground.

His helmet popped off and landed at the running back's feet. The helmet exploded early. It was so powerful that it propelled the running back up in the air several feet carrying him into the end zone. Our team won. The Tel Aviv players were furious. They tried to get a penalty for an illegal trick play. Fortunately for us, no penalty was called. The play was upheld. Although it was a botched attempt at terror, Mosheik was hailed as a hero. The Pigskins were so amused at Mosheik's antics, that they let him into the group. Soon thereafter, he went on a bombing spree. He bombed football shops all over the Middle East and Europe. He was on Interpol's most wanted list. He was caught and almost jailed in England. However, the royal princess fell in love with him. He's the perfect combination of madness and beauty. He's a delicious criminal. He's hard to resist. Anyhow, he exploited the princess' love and escaped to America. Now he's on the loose determined to complete his mission which is to destroy American football and America along with it."

Russell sat back in his chair twirling his pen. He then looked at Bonnie and said, "We need to catch this guy and fast. Football season is about to end. The word on the street is that he's planning something big. He was arrested in New York for streaking at one of their football games. They let him go because he didn't have an I.D. I guess we'll start looking for him there."

Russell and Bonnie staked out an apartment in Brooklyn. It was the place of a known member of The Pigskins. It was early in the morning. Russell bought some doughnuts and coffee from a nearby shop. Russell said to Bonnie, "Have a doughnut. I have glazed, jelly, chocolate and coconut." Bonnie replied, "I'll just have coffee." Russell commented, "Come on, have a doughnut. You're skin and bones. Don't tell me you're an ex-supermodel." Bonnie replied sluggishly, "Actually, I'm an ex-Miss Saudi Arabia." Russell replied, "Oh!" Bonnie continued, "I hope I'm not being rude. I'm just not hungry. I have a strong desire burning in my bones. I'm eager to see Mosheik. I think I'm still in love with him." Russell said to her in a serious tone, "You know if we catch him, he's going to prison for a long time." Bonnie answered sadly, "Yes, I know."

It was after lunchtime when Russell said to

Bonnie excitedly, "Look! There's Mosheik's old neighbor. We need to question him. I'm sure he knows where Mosheik is hiding and what his big plan is." Bonnie said to Russell, "I'll question him. I'm an expert at it." Russell said to her, "Be careful. These are dangerous people." Bonnie entered the building. She struck up a conversation with Mosheik's friend. His name was Omar. Omar invited her into his place. She agreed. It soon became dark. Russell could see Bonnie's silhouette against the window. He saw her drop the trench coat and embrace Omar. They then dropped out of view. The next afternoon, Bonnie returned to the car with Russell. She sat next to him looking out with a naughty look on her face. Russell asked her, "Well, it's been twenty four hours. What did he say?" Bonnie answered, "I got nothing." Russell squinted his eyes at her and said, "From the look on your face, I think you got something. By the way, what are you wearing under that trench coat?" Russell opened her coat and said in amazement, "Oh no! Nothing but Russian, I mean Arabian beauty. You're supposed to be carrying a weapon and a badge." Bonnie replied, "I have them in my pockets." Russell then said, "Let's go back in there and get him. This time we'll take him to headquarters and question him American style."

Russell pounded on the door and yelled, "Open up, Federal Agents!" They then heard Omar scuffling around in the apartment. Russell kicked the door open and shouted, "Freeze or I'll shoot!" Omar pulled out a weapon and fired several shots. Bonnie fired back. The shot knocked the gun out of Omar's hand. Omar darted for the window in an attempt to escape. Before he could reach the window, Russell got his arms around Omar's knees tackling him to the ground. Bonnie slapped handcuffs around his wrists. She then pulled his head back by the hair and gave him a deep, passionate, kiss. She then said to Russell, "That was exciting." Russell replied, "I'm sure it was."

At headquarters, Russell slammed his fist on the table and yelled, "Where is he? I want to know where he is! Give us Mosheik! Omar answered infallibly, "I won't rat out a brother. We are Pig Skins. Hear us squeal. Oink, Oink!" Russell looked at him indignantly and said, "You know what I have here Omar?" Omar nodded his head no. Russell explained, "This is a bowl of mud. Eat it you pig! Eat!" Russell shoved his face into the mud. He then said, "Wallow in it! I know you love it. It's your favorite. It's mud pie. Eat!" Bonnie opened the door and said, "Russell may I see you for a moment." Russell stepped out of the room. He said to Bonnie, "Okay, I've played bad cop. Now you go in there and play good cop." Bonnie smiled. Before she went in, Russell stopped her and said, "Here, give him a drink of water. It's laced with truth serum." Bonnie smiled again and went into the room with Omar. She said, "Please excuse my partner. He's an American investigator. His methods are harsh and barbaric. Here have some water. You must be thirsty." Omar took the glass and chugged down the water. Bonnie got close to Omar and spoke into his ear, "Now tell me, where's Mosheik?" Omar answered, "He's somewhere in California. He's planning something big at the Tulip Bowl." Suddenly, Ed entered the room and said, "Bonnie, Mosheik has sent us a message via Skype." Ed, Russell and Bonnie listened to the message. Mosheik said, "I hear you're looking for me. Well, it's too late. Soon, I will execute my plan and destroy America. My people will be free from American influence. We will then dominate the world." Bonnie interrupted and said, "Mosheik my beloved don't do this." Mosheik responded with astonishment, "Bahijah? It is really you? But of course, I'd know those pom-poms anywhere." Bonnie replied excitedly, "You noticed." Mosheik said to Bonnie, "Yes, I did notice. I've always loved you. It's just that in my line of work; it's business before pleasure." Bonnie replied dramatically, "You don't have to do this Mosheik. We can go back to the homeland and live a life together." Mosheik replied, "No beloved! It's too late. I believe what I believe. I can't turn back now. Goodbye my friend." Ed, Russell and Bonnie looked at each other in silence as they pondered the message in the video. Then, Ed spoke. He said, "Okay! We know he hates football. We know he's planning something big. We know he's checking out the Tulip Bowl. Let's keep investigating and find out what exactly he's up to." Russell spoke next. He said, "I'll have Kristi and Joel out on the street. Bonnie and I will continue questioning Omar. Hopefully, we'll be able to get more out of him." Ed replied, "Sounds good. Keep me informed." As she was looking at Omar through the one way glass, Bonnie said, "I must sleep with him. Once I wrap myself around this deranged criminal, he'll talk to me." Ed and Russell looked at each other and said, "Oh brother!"

Kristi and Joel walked the beat searching the sports shops. Kristi showed Mosheik's photograph to one of the store managers. He said, "I saw this guy in here the other day. He bought all our footballs. I had to order some more. They should be in later today." The next day, Kristi and Joel went to a football game. Joel said, "Nothing more exciting than a gridiron football game." Kristi sat close to Joel. She curled her arm around his and leaned her head on his shoulder. She then said, "Thanks for being my partner on this investigation." Joel turned to her and said, "I've always wanted to work with you Kristi. I've had a crush on you for a long time. We'll talk about it later. For now, let's enjoy the game."

Before the halftime show began, Mosheik streaked down the field wearing no clothes. He was wearing only a pig snout and dark, rimmed, glasses with no lenses. It was a disguise that identified him as a member of the radical group the Pig Skins.

He stood on the platform grabbed the microphone and said, "I am Hadan Mosheik world renowned terrorist. You've probably seen me on the hit show, "Bad Boys Most Wanted". I'm here to announce the demise of American football. Football is nothing more than a false god sitting on the throne of world commerce. You've heard the saying, "Money can't buy you love". It was also a hit song by the Beatles, by the way. Well, football can't bring you happiness. Football only creates an illusionary happiness. No my friends, true happiness only comes by having lunch with good people. Not with people who sit you on a hard wooden bar stool then forget about you. But, I digress. Our mission is to destroy football so that Ishtar can take her rightful throne. Ishtar will rise again to rule with beauty and grace throughout the land. I will be her king and father many children with her. Long live Ishtar! Long live happiness! I will now destroy football." One of Mosheik's henchmen handed him a device. Mosheik flew in a pair of blimps over the stadium. The blimps were loaded with deadly cobras. Suddenly, it began to rain. Mosheik said in astonishment, "Where did this rain come from? Rain wasn't in the forecast. Brrrr! The rain sure is cold. Oh no! This means the whole world will see little Mosheik shrink. Quick! Somebody get me a raincoat." One of Mosheik's henchmen said, "We didn't bring any, Mo." Mosheik said to himself, "I've been publicly humiliated." He then addressed the crowd with a loud cry, "I'll have my revenge!" Before he could drop the cobras on the crowd, lightning flashed blowing up the blimps. The snakes were burnt to ashes." Mosheik yelped, "Yikes!" Mosheik and his men ran for safety. Kristi and Joel went after them fighting through a crowd of panicked people.

Mosheik put on some clothes and got into a getaway car with one of his henchmen. Kristi ran after the car. She jumped on to it and held on to the hood. She looked through the windshield and said, "Stop the car! I'm a federal agent. Mosheik is under arrest." The driver maneuvered the car in order to shake her off. Joel jumped on to the back of a truck. It was driving parallel to Mosheik. Joel commanded, "Stop the car or I'll shoot!" Before Joel could shoot, he lost balance and dropped the gun. He then fell off the truck when Mosheik's car hit it while attempting to shake off Kristi. Kristi let go and fell on to the street. She rolled off the road narrowly escaping getting run over. She stopped near Joel.

Russell and Bonnie stopped at the hospital to check on Joel and Kristi. Russell said to Bonnie, "The doctor said that they're both fine. They'll just need time to heal." Kristi motioned to Russell. Russell said to her, "Don't wear yourself out Kristi. You need to save your strength. You have a lot of healing to do. Write it down on my notepad." Kristi wrote, "Mosheik is buying up every football in town. He might be using them as part of his big plan. Speaking of big, Mosheik is one very healthy terrorist." Bonnie replied jealously, "Watch your language you little slut. Mosheik is my man. Only I get access to his healthy, manly, body." Russell interrupted her, "Leave her alone Bonnie. She's hurt." Bonnie flicked her head and stormed out of the room. Russell said to Kristi and Joel, "Get well soon both of you. I need you back at work as soon as possible." Russell went outside and met with Bonnie. Bonnie was on her phone. She said to Russell, "My Russian friends just told me that Mosheik has created a football bomb. He's going to pass out footballs to as many spectators as possible throughout the Tulip Bowl. At halftime, while the blimp is directly over the stadium, he'll detonate it along with all the footballs creating an explosion that will wipe out several blocks." Russell replied, "Sweet Sister Bonnie! It'll be the end of football as we know it. We have to stop him and fast. Quick! Let's go to the Tulip Bowl." Russell and Bonnie got into the black F.B.I. car. They raced down the streets of Pasadena in pursuit of a madman.

Russell spotted a man near a sports utility vehicle hooking up a small trailer filled with footballs. He was wearing sports garb along with the infamous pig snout glasses. Russell cried out, "There he is Bonnie! Hold on!" Russell made a sharp U-turn. Mosheik jumped into the sports utility vehicle and drove off. The chase let to the highway. F.B.I. and police cars piled up behind Mosheik. Russell was in the lead car. He said to Bonnie, "Call him. Maybe he'll give himself up." Bonnie called Mosheik. She said, "Give yourself up Mosheik. Every cop in the country is on your tail. You can't escape. When you get out of prison, I'll be waiting for you my lover. We can live the rest of our lives together just you and me my king." Mosheik replied, "I can't stop now Bahijah. Babylon will rise again. However, before that can happen, Ishtar must reclaim her rightful throne. Sorry my beauty. I'll see you in paradise." Bonnie with tears in her eyes said, "No matter what happens, I just want you to know that I love you." Russell called the officers ahead. He instructed them to set up a road block. He said, "No matter what, don't let him get near the Tulip Bowl" Mosheik saw the road block and drove through it. The spikes blew out the tires. Mosheik lost control of the vehicle. He went barreling toward a nearby church.

Billy Jo Cool got up early. He went out for his regular morning run. When he finished his run, he sat at the table for breakfast. He had pigs in a blanket with a side of waffles along with toast and coffee. After breakfast, he showered and cleaned up. He prepared his notes for the presentation. He then put on his priestly garb and entered the church. He presented to the congregation a fiery sermon titled, "Will There Be Football in Heaven?" After the sermon, Billy Jo's wife, Violet, led the congregation in prayer. She began with the whole congregation repeating, "Hail Mary Full of Grace the Lord is with you. Blessed are you among women…"

Suddenly, Mosheik crashed into the church. The footballs in the trailer exploded. The church was demolished. Everyone died including Mosheik, Russell, and Bonnie. It was called, "The Hail Mary Tragedy". On a bright note, there was one survivor. It was Billy Jo's son Jo Cool.

Jo Cool lost his parents at the tender age of five. He spent five years at a foster home. The house manager's name was Linda Flora. The foster kids called her Miss Flower. She worked night and day trying to find a loving family for all her foster kids. In the meantime, the foster kids at the home were a special family of their own.

One day, a biker couple stopped by to drop off gifts for Christmas. Road Hog and Easy Ride noticed Jo Cool playing with the other children. They said to Miss Flower, "Who's that little boy? He has nice hair. Look at those side burns. He looks like a little James Dean. We'd like to adopt him." Miss Flower replied, "I'll get the paperwork ready right away." After the New Year, Jo Cool became the son of the biker couple Road Hog and Easy Ride.

They lived like gypsies going from town to town. They lived life care free enjoying the freedom of the open road. Jo Cool rode with bikers throughout his youth.

Jo Cool grew up to be a very handsome young man. He became quite popular with the ladies. Every girl in the county wanted to be Jo Cool's girlfriend. He wore a t-shirt, leather jacket, blue jeans, & biker boots. He rode a fat boy chopper. He rode it Marlon Brando style. One day while passing through Pasadena, a group of cheerleaders gathered around his bike. Jo looked at the head cheerleader. Her name was Sandy. He shook his head at her to get on the bike. Sandy's arms rose up in front of her as she took slow, small, steps toward him. She said to the other cheerleaders, "Why am I being drawn toward him? Help, Ladies!" The other girls were transfixed on Jo. They all said together, "You are so cool!" Sandy got on the bike, put her arms around Jo and whispered into his ear, "You are so cool." Jo took her to lover's lane. There they could overlook the city and enjoy the scenery as well as each other. They kissed and kissed and kissed. The next time they went out Jo took Sandy to a football game. It was an action packed butte of a game. While the players were playing, Jo said to Sandy, "If my parents hadn't passed away, I'd probably be playing football today. Unfortunately, being cool like I am, I don't quite fit in with normal people. I guess football is out of the question." Sandy looked at Jo and said, "You are so cool." Then, they kissed and kissed and kissed.

At the start of the summer, Jo met with Sandy for the last time. They had a fun time at the beach. They came out of the water after noon. They kissed, on the beach, as the waves came in around them. Sandy looked down at Jo and said, "It would be nice if you could stay. You could come to school and play football. Jo replied, "I can't. I've been here too long. You're a special girl that's why I stayed a while. However, a biker lives his life on the road. He just comes and goes like the waves. No Sandy, I've been here too long." Sandy asked, "Where will you go?" Jo responded, "I don't know. A biker goes with the road. I guess I'll go where the road leads me. Hopefully, I'll catch up with my biker family and continue living life riding the road." Jo changed into some dry clothes, got on his bike and gave

Sandy one last kiss. He then drove his bike along the beach until he got back to the road." Sandy waved at him and said, "You are so cool."

The next day, Jo stopped at a general store. As he pulled up, he asked some girls standing outside wearing Daisy Duke's, "Is it okay if I use the can?" The girls all replied, "You are so cool." Jo responded, "I'll take that as a yes." While Jo was using the facilities, two hell's angels rode in and robbed the store. They killed the store owner and scared the girls away. Jo came out of the restroom and was about to ride away. Before he kick started his bike, he decided to have lunch in the general store. He went inside. As soon as he entered the store, he said, "Mother Mary! What the hell happened here?" Jo made his way around the mess. He saw the store owner lying on the floor behind the counter. He said, "Ben! Hold On! I'm coming!" Jo turned Ben over to see if he was still alive. There was blood everywhere. Jo's hands got covered in blood. While Jo was trying to help Ben, the sheriff showed up. He said to Jo, "Get your hands up partner! Don't move you criminal! You're under arrest." Jo responded, "You don't understand. I didn't do anything. I was just trying to help. You have the wrong man." The sheriff replied, "We'll let the judge decide that." The sheriff handcuffed Jo and took him to jail.

At trial, Jo was assigned a court appointed attorney. She was an ex-hooker turned lawyer. Her name was Raspberry Treat. She traveled from the big city to the one horse town of Blahville. She was sexy, curvy, and young. Whenever she would pass by, the men of Blahville would say, "You are so sexy." She was eager and ready to defend her client in the battlefield called The Courtroom. She sat next to Jo. She turned to him, extended her hand, and said, "Hi, I'm Miss Treat. I'll be your attorney." Jo showed her the handcuffs and said, "I'm sorry but I can't shake your hand. I'm tied up at the moment." Raspberry looked at the handcuffs then said, "Oh, sorry about that." She then looked up at Jo. As soon as she got a good look at him, she said, "You are so cool."

The prosecutor slammed Jo. He brought up every little detail from Jo's past. He made Jo look like a common criminal. He said to the jury, "Bikers are nothing more than criminals with sideburns. They ride the open road carefree raping and violating society with their in your face attitude. Imagine killing a store owner; Ben our friend; Ben a respected member of the community; over some boar jerky. I would ask you to give him the chair. However, the maximum is life. I hope you do the right thing and send this rebel to prison." The members of the jury looked at Jo and said, "You are so cool."

Jo looked at Raspberry and said, "Shouldn't you be defending me or something? That guy is having me for lunch." Raspberry said, "Why are my knees knocking? Why is my body tingling? I'm not nervous or anything." Before she stood up to address the jury, she turned and looked at Jo. As soon as she looked at him, she gave out a violent scream and fell to the ground. Her body was quivering and convulsing. The bailiff ran up to her to help. He turned over to Judge Margaret and said, "I believe she just had an orgasm." Jo cried out, "Hey! I didn't touch her." Then Jo said to Judge Margaret, "Your honor isn't this grounds for a mistrial?" Judge Margaret replied, "Hold on Jo. Curtis, take Miss Treat out for a drink of water and some fresh air." She then turned to Jo and said, "I'm sorry Jo. I can't seem to find a lawyer for you.

The male lawyers are intimidated by your coolness. The lady lawyers, as you just saw, go batty. I have no choice but to send you to prison.

The prisoners gathered together for the annual summer show. Jo had been in prison for a while. He met some talented friends. By coincidence, they were all bike riders. They put together an act and performed at the show. They performed Elvis', "Jailhouse Rock". Jo had the Elvis look and swagger down to the letter. The prisoners all said together, "You are so cool." Jo became the coolest prisoner in the prison. Jo rocked. Jo's coolness caught the attention of the warden.

One day, Jo was in the prison yard with his buddies. One of the prisoners, his name was Pester, walked up to Jo, shoved him and said, "I don't like you sideburns." Jo responded, "Hey! Cool it! Don't you know who I am? I'm Jo Cool the coolest prisoner in the prison." Pester replied, "You don't look so cool to me." He then swung at Jo. Jo ducked. He ran over to some of the prisoners playing football. He grabbed the football away from the quarterback and threw it at Pester. It was a direct hit to the chops. Pester went down. He was out cold for a few seconds. He got up in a daze and went after Jo. He said angrily, "I'm gonna throw you around the field like that football you punk." The guards came in, handcuffed Pester and took him away.

Johnny, the quarterback, said to Jo, "You have a nice arm there buddy. How about you play some football with us? Jo answered hesitantly, "Okay!" Johnny said to him, "You can be quarterback for the yellow team." The prisoners & guards were gambling on the game. The blue team was heavily favored. The teams began to play. Every time Jo got the ball, he threw a touchdown. The yellow team won in a blowout victory. The warden saw the whole thing from the watchtower.

The warden entered the conference room. He was there to discuss the prison's economic shortfalls with the committee. He said, "If we don't raise some money quick, we'll have to shut down the prison. It'll be a huge loss for Blahville. The prison is a major employer here in town. Also, it'll ruin my chances at running for mayor. We need to do something fast." He then asked, "Any ideas out there?" The members of the committee stared at him in silence. The warden broke the silence by saying, "Here's my proposal in one word, 'Football'. We can put together a football team for the Blahville prison. We can then play the other prisons in the state. The two teams with the best records can play in a championship game. Football will help us raise enough money to keep the prison operating for a long time." The members of the committee agreed.

The Blahville prison football team was assembled. They were called the Warthogs. They got into trouble early on in the season. The warden said to Coach Waver, "We've lost six games in a row. Nobody will buy tickets to see a losing team. We'll need to win the remaining ten games without losing one in order to have a shot at the championship. What's wrong coach? How can we turn this thing around?" Coach Waver replied, "We have as good a team as anybody else. However, what we desperately need is a good quarterback." The warden remarked, "A quarterback?" Coach Waver answered, "Yes, the team needs someone they can look up to. They need a leader on the field. It'll require someone with lots of coolness. However, where are we going to find such a person in Blahville?" The warden responded, "I think I know someone that fits the bill, coach."

Jo was called in to the warden's office. The warden said to Jo, "I saw you play ball with the prisoners a while back. You have a very good arm. I'd like for you to play for my team the Warthogs." Jo replied, "Don't I have to be a prison guard to play for the team? Besides, what you saw was just a friendly game among prisoners. I have no experience." The warden smiled and said, "You leave that to me. I'll make sure you're ready." Jo was assigned a quarterback coach. He was also given access to the gym in order to train.

It was game time. Jo suited up and went out to the field. It was the Warthogs vs. Tigers. The team lined up. Jo called for the snap. He got the ball and ran right. He threw downfield to the receiver. The pass was intercepted. Throughout the entire first half, Jo was intercepted. At halftime, Jo said to Coach Waver, "Maybe I'm not so cool after all. Have I been living a lie? Have I been an average Jo all this time and not know it? I'm sorry coach for wasting your time. You better find another quarterback." Coach Waver replied, "A famous coach once said,

'It ain't over till it's over.' The true mark of coolness is poise under adversity. A cool Jo doesn't leave a job half done. Now go out there and lead this team to victory like I know you can." Jo looked at Coach Waver and said, "You are so cool."

The Warthogs were down twenty one to zero. In the huddle, Jo told the guys, "Let's run an End Around. I saw it in one of the videos while training." The guys responded, "Huh?" Jo explained, "When I get the ball, everyone run to the right." The team lined up. Jo called for the ball. As soon as the ball was snapped, everyone moved to the right as well as the Tiger defense. As a result, the left side of the field was wide open. Jo ran all the way to the end zone. The team sprang to life. The Warthog defense then held the offense. The Warthog offense lined up. Jo called for the ball. This time Jo stayed in the pocket looking downfield. Before getting tackled, Jo threw a bullet pass right down the middle. The ball passed through the hands of two defenders one standing behind the other. It was like thread going through the eye of a needle. The ball hit the wide receiver right in the numbers. He caught the ball and sprinted for the end zone. On the next possession, the Tigers were about to score. It would have put the game out of reach and broken the will of the Warthogs. However, the Tigers, who were just about to score, fumbled the ball. The defense scooped it up and ran it all the way back for a Warthog touchdown. The coach called the team to the sideline. He said, "We don't have much time left. Let's stay calm and not fumble. Keep your hands on the ball." The Warthogs lined up. Jo called for the ball. He then handed it to the running back. He picked up only a yard. Jo handed off the ball again and again. It was fourth down. There was time for only one more play. The Warthogs lined up for a field goal. Jo would hold the ball for the kicker. It would be a fifty four yard attempt. Jo called for the ball. Instead of holding it for the kicker, Jo attempted a pass. It was a fake field goal trick play. Jo ran to the right. He dodged a defender then another. Jo ran left across the field. He then threw the ball down field to a wide open wide receiver. He caught the ball without having to stop. The Warthogs won twenty seven to twenty one. The Warthogs won the rest of their games. As a result, they made it to the championship game.

They were matched up against the heavily favored Rhinos. Again, the Warthogs came from behind scoring three touchdowns to tie the game. Then, the Rhinos scored a field goal. The team celebrated on the sideline as if victory was secure. The Warthogs lined up. Jo called for the ball. He handed the ball to the running back. Before getting tackled, he lateralled to Jo. Jo ran left. He dodged a tackle. He then ran right across the field. He threw deep downfield to the wide receiver. He caught the ball and ran it to the end zone. The Warthogs won the championship. The prison celebrated. There was even a small article about it in the Blahville paper. The warden's idea was a huge success. The prison had more than enough money with plenty to spare.

The Blahville Javelinas, a football team for Blahville College, was just a dream for athletic director Willie Hope. He said to the school administrator at a meeting, "This College needs a football team. A college without one isn't taken seriously. Anyhow, we need something to boost morale around here. Football is a great morale booster. It'll also give the kids at this school a reason to be proud of being Javelinas." Mr. Thrifty, the administrator, said, "Yes, I agree. It's about time this school gets a football team."

The warden called Jo to his office. He said, "Jo, I have some good news and some better news. First, the bikers that killed Ben, the store owner, have been caught. They confessed to the crime. You're a free man. Next, Coach Lavish, a friend of mine, is putting together a football team for the Javelinas. He was at the championship game against the Rhinos. He wants you to be his quarterback." Jo responded, "What is it with this town and football? Besides, don't I have to be a high school grad to play college ball? I've never been to high school." The warden looked at Jo and said, "Football is a way of life around here. As far as high school, you leave that to me. You just get ready to play ball." Jo was given a special G.E.D. exam for bikers.

The Javelinas were up against the Matadors. They were getting clobbered. Steve Canon, the first string quarterback, got injured. The doctor told Coach Lavish, "He'll be out the whole season." Coach Lavish called out to Jo, "Okay Jo, you're our man. Go out there and win." When Jo ran out onto the field, the cheerleaders cheered, "Who's the coolest guy of all? The one who knows how to throw the ball; Jo! Jo! Jo! Yea, Jo!" The crowd cheered along with the girls. In the huddle, Jo instructed the guys, "Let's do the Dead Man." The team lined up. Jo called for the ball. The receiver ran deep and fast. Suddenly, he pretended like the play was over. As soon as the defender moved out of the way, Jo passed him the ball. It was a quick score. On the next possession, Jo called for the Statue of Liberty play. The ball was snapped. Jo pump faked a throw. Instead, he handed off to the running back. The running back swerved and cut across players into open territory. He ran it all the way for a touchdown. The crowd got into the excitement. They all said with one voice to Jo the quarterback, "You are so cool." On the kick return, the Matadors fumbled. The Javelinas picked it up and ran it for a touchdown. On the next possession, the Matadors threw an interception. The offense came out and lined up. Jo called for the ball. He ran right, dodged a defender, and ran back to the middle. He threw straight downfield to the receiver. He caught the ball and ran it for a touchdown. The Javelinas won twenty eight to twenty four. The Javelinas went undefeated the entire season. As a result, they made it to the championship game. It was the Javelinas vs. Badgers in the Tulip Bowl. The school was so excited; it held a special championship pep rally. Everyone knew that it was Jo Cool's throwing arm that carried the Javelinas to the championship.

It was soon game time. The arena was packed. It was sold out. It was also televised on prime time. All eyes were on the Cinderella team of the year, the Blahville Javelinas. The two teams met at mid-field prepared for battle. The Badgers won the coin toss. The game began. The Badgers were at their twenty yard line. The Javelina defense came out and held strong. Then, the Javelina offense took the field. The Badgers defensive coach said to his guys, "Jo Cool is the "coolest quarterback in college ball. He'll kill us out there. We need to trip him up and slow him down. If we can take him out, this game is ours. Now go out there and stop him." On third down, the Badgers put on the blitz. Jo was tackled hard to the ground. Every bone in his body ached. It was the first time Jo had been sacked. At the side line, Jo told Coach Lavish, "Coach, I don't think I like football anymore. I quit." Coach Lavish responded, "What? You're telling me this now." He thought for a few seconds then said, "You know Jo coolness can sometimes take you places you never expected. Your coolness has brought you to the brink of greatness. When I say greatness, I don't mean being on the cover of a magazine, or winning a trophy, or championship ring. True greatness Jo is just being cool. Are you cool Jo?" Jo responded with a shout, "Yeah" Coach Lavish replied, "Then go back out there, win or lose, and be cool." The Badgers marched fifty five yards on the ground for a touchdown. In the huddle, Jo told his guys, "You all realize we're not supposed to be here. Nothing exciting ever happens in Blahville. Nevertheless, we're here. Let's give it everything we've got. Hitch and go guys."

The Javelinas lined up. Jo called for the ball. He pump faked then threw deep for a quick touchdown. The Badgers marched downfield again on the ground. They scored a field goal. At half time, the cheerleaders and dance squad put on a show for Jo Cool. At the end of the show the entire arena cried out with one voice, "You are so cool!"

At the start of the second half, the Badgers

marched downfield on the ground to score a field goal. On the next possession, Jo called for the Fumblerooski play. The offense fumbled the ball Jo pretended to run with it. He then faked a handoff to the running back. The Badger defense went after the running back. In the meantime, the offensive guard picked up the ball and ran it in for a touchdown. The crowd roared with euphoria as the Javelinas took the lead fourteen to thirteen. The Badger offense came back out to the field. They marched all the way to the end zone on the ground. It was now twenty to fourteen. The Javelinas took the field again. Jo called for the Flea Flicker. He handed off to the running back. Before getting tackled, the running back tossed the ball back to Jo. Jo threw deep downfield to the receiver for an easy touchdown. The crowd again roared loud as the Javelinas took the lead. On the next series, the Badgers marched downfield on the ground. They scored a field goal. The score was twenty three to twenty one. The Javelina offense went out to the field. In the huddle, Jo said, "We only have time for one more play. We're out of field goal range. The defense is too strong and ready for a running play. We have only one choice, the Hail Mary." The guys responded, "The Hail Mary has only been done once before. It was in the classic Raiders vs. Sentinels game." Jo replied, I know. It's our only chance. We may never be in a championship game again." The guys agreed. The team lined up. Jo called for the ball. He ran to the right. He dodged a defender, turned around, and ran left. He narrowly escaped the hands of a tackler then bounced off of another. He continued to run left buying time for his receivers. Then, Jo threw deep downfield with no time remaining. It was a high pass with a beautiful arch. The receiver caught it without having to stop his sprint. He ran it all the way to the end zone. The crowd roared. It was pandemonium. Coach Lavish came out on to the field and said to Jo, "Wow! That sure was beautiful. It was the best pass I've ever seen. It would have made history for sure. Too bad you stepped out of bounds." He then smiled at Jo and said, "Let's go congratulate the Badgers on their championship win."

During the off season, Jo Cool got bored with college and quit. He rejoined his biker family. He has never been seen since. The Blahville Javelinas never had a winning season after the Tulip Bowl. However, the people of this humble town still talk about Jo Cool and the championship game. It was the most exciting game we ever lost.

Printed in the United States
By Bookmasters